W9-ASF-114

"Babies are a big drag, let me tell you," Libby said.

Libby should know what she's talking about. She has a baby in her family who's just one and a half years old. She twists heads off Libby's dolls if she gets her hands on them, scribbles on the table with a crayon if you leave one lying around, steals toothbrushes just because she likes to go around sucking on them, eats pennies and won't let you take them out of her mouth. (Once she had *nine* pennies in there—we counted.) Libby says she's the bane of her existence.

Other Bullseye Books you will enjoy

The Kid in the Red Jacket by Barbara Park
Lucy Forever and Miss Rosetree, Shrinks by Susan Shreve
The Secret Life of the Underwear Champ by Betty Miles
There's a Boy in the Girls' Bathroom by Louis Sachar
Witch Week by Diana Wynne Jones

DR. M. JERRY WEISS, Distinguished Service Professor of Communications at Jersey City State College, is the educational consultant for Bullseye Books. Currently Chair of the International Reading Association President's Advisory Committee on Intellectual Freedom, he travels frequently to give workshops on the use of trade books in schools.

Confessions Of An Only Child

Norma Klein

Illustrated by Richard Cuffari

Bullseye Books · Alfred A. Knopf
New York

ST. PHILIP'S COLLEGE LIBRARY

A Bullseye Book
Published by Alfred A. Knopf, Inc.

Text copyright © 1974 by Norma Klein.
Illustrations copyright © 1974 by Random House, Inc.
Cover art copyright © 1988 by Deborah Chabrian.

All rights reserved under International and Pan-American Copyright
Conventions. Published in the United States by Alfred A. Knopf, Inc.,
New York, and simultaneously in Canada by Random House of
Canada Limited, Toronto. Distributed by Random House, Inc., New
York. Originally published in hardcover in 1974 by Pantheon Books,
a division of Random House, Inc.

Library of Congress Catalog Card Number: 73-14750
ISBN: 0-394-80569-0
RL: 4.5

Manufactured in the United States of America
0 1 2 3 4 5 6 7 8 9

*For Missy, Alva, Bruce and Teddy
and, of course,
Camille and Charlie*

CONTENTS

Confessions
Of An
Only Child

I

Libby,
Me,
and Rosabelle Franklin

"Boy, your mother's getting really fat!" Libby said. "She's gigantic."

"She's not fat, dope," I said. "She's pregnant."

"Well, she sure looks fat."

"That's just the baby inside her. When it's born, she'll be regular again."

Libby and me were peeking in at Mom who was sleeping in the bedroom. Monday is Libby's day to visit me because school gets out at two instead of three the way it usually does. Some Mondays I go visit her. Mom had

3

ST. PHILIP'S COLLEGE LIBRARY

let us in and then went off to the bedroom. There she was sound asleep with Elvira sleeping right on top of her stomach, like a kitten on top of a haystack. Elvira is one of our dogs. She's quite old, actually, since Mom had her even before she married Dad. She's a Yorkshire terrier and very small and usually quite grumpy. Mom loves her, however. Dad and I like William better. He's a German shorthaired pointer, and he's only nine months old. He and Elvira get along all right, but sometimes Elvira gets really mad at William and he slinks away under the couch. Dad says he just has high spirits because he's a pup. It's hard to imagine Elvira *ever* having high spirits.

In my room Libby and me began playing with my Indian tent. Mom got it for me last week when I went to have a filling done at the dentist. She said if I was good, I could have it. It's really great. Lib and I play all kinds of camping and sleeping over games. We use some of the doll house people in it too.

"You know, you're really going to have trouble," Libby said, sighing. "I feel sorry for you."

"What about?"

"That baby will just drive you crazy. How come they're having one?"

"Just wanted to, I guess."

"When's it coming?"

"June, around my birthday." I'll be nine in June. Libby will be nine this month. She was late. She was supposed to be born in February, but she just wouldn't come

4

ST. PHILIP'S COLLEGE LIBRARY

out. I was early. I guess I just got tired of sitting in there with nothing to do.

"Babies are a big drag, let me tell you," Libby said.

Libby should know what she's talking about. She has a baby in her family, Baby Matilda, who's just one and a half years old. Sometimes Lib and me call her B.M. because she stinks so much if she has something in her diaper. Libby's mother doesn't think that's nice, but we always say it's short for Baby Matilda. B.M. does some really terrible things. She twists heads off Libby's doll house dolls if she gets her hands on them, scribbles on the table with a crayon or a dri mark pen if you leave one lying around, steals toothbrushes just because she likes to go around sucking on them, breaks china cups from a beautiful set of china Libby got for her seventh birthday, eats pennies and won't let you take them out of her mouth. (Once she had *nine* pennies in there—we counted.) Those are just things she does regularly, every day things. Sometimes she's even worse. Like Libby said the other morning she opened up this jar of Vaseline and smeared it all over everything—her dress, her legs, and even her *face*. It was really *disgusting*. The other thing is she's not very smart. She knows about one word or maybe two, "doggie" and "baba" for bottle. So you can't talk to her or explain stuff to her or anything. She babbles all the time, but it doesn't make *any* sense. Libby says she's the bane of her existence. (That's an expression meaning someone who's a terrible pest that our teacher

5

in school, Miss Ross, is always saying about this boy, Jimmy Elgin.)

Whenever I visit Libby's house after school, the first thing we have to do is climb on top of her bunk bed where B.M. can't get us. We stay there all afternoon, playing and watching TV. If we want a toy, we let out a yell and Libby's mother hands it up to us. We can even eat up there—Libby has a red tray that you can have snacks on. Once an awful thing *almost* happened. We looked down and there was Baby Matilda climbing up the ladder to the top of the bunk bed! She was about halfway up, hanging on like a leech. Libby let out a loud shriek and her mother came running in and snatched Baby Matilda off. Boy, that would be terrible! If Baby Matilda ever learns to climb up to the top of that ladder, I don't know *what* we'll do. I don't think she will though, till she's three or four or so.

"You know what I'd like to be?" I said to Libby.

"A ballet dancer?"

"No, not like that . . . I'd like to always be an only child."

"Wouldn't that be great?"

There are some only children I know. Ida's an only child. That's because her mother is divorced and can't have more babies. But if she gets married again, maybe she will. Anyway, right now Ida's house is always nice and peaceful. I like Libby better—she's my best friend—but it is more peaceful at Ida's house. Michael's an only

6

child too. Both his parents work and his mother says she hasn't the time or the money. It's funny. Mom and Dad are always saying "Poor thing, he's an only child," as though it were so terrible. I don't see anything so terrible about it at all. I think it's wonderful.

"You'd better not have a boy," Libby said.

"Why not?" I asked.

"Because they do this really awful thing," Libby said. "I saw it at my cousin's house. When you're changing their diaper they pee right up in the air, in your eye even, if you don't look out."

I made a face. "Ugh."

"It's pretty bad," Libby said. "Girls at least pee straight down."

We played awhile and then went into Mom and Dad's bedroom to watch TV. By then Mom was sitting up and yawning. "Oh Lordy," she said. "I was out like a light."

Grownups use such funny expressions. I have a book where I write them down. Like "I'm going to blow my stack" or "You'd better be all ears" and things like that.

"Hey Mom, it's TV time," I said.

"Oh . . . well, do you girls want milk and cookies and stuff?"

"Sure . . . want some chocolate chips, Lib?"

"Umm," Libby said. She was kicking off her shoes and crawling up on the bed. You have to be careful with cookies or William will eat them. He's the type of dog

7

that's *always* hungry. I guess he can't help it. Libby and I lay down on Mom and Dad's big bed and watched TV. We put the cookie plate up there with us. Then we began jumping up and down on the bed, singing, "Rosabelle Franklin, yeah, yeah, yeah!" Dad doesn't like us to jump up and down on the bed. He says it's bad for the bed. But Mom lets us when he's not around.

Taking our cookie plate which was bouncing around too, Mom said, "It's not Rosabelle Franklin, Toe . . . it's Roose*velt* Franklin. He's named after a president. Anyway, Rosabelle couldn't be a boy's name."

"Yes, it could," I said. "Anyway, I like Rosabelle better!"

"Well, you listen next time they say it on TV and you'll hear it's really Roosevelt Franklin."

I always do listen and to me it sounds like Rosa*belle*. That's a prettier name anyway.

Pretty soon Libby's mother came to pick her up. She's friends with Mom. They have tea while we play, but at five thirty, her mother always says "Okay, Lib, time to set off." That's when Libby and me hide. They can never find us. Libby's mother and Mom go all over the house looking for us. They open closet doors and look under tables, but they *never* find us. This time we hid in the bathtub and pulled the shower curtain around so they couldn't see. They probably *wouldn't* have ever found us except William came poking in and gave us away.

Mom and me went down to walk William and Elvira while Libby's mother and she went to get a cab. I always walk William. He's big, but I can manage him because I'm very strong for my age. Elvira goes without her leash.

"See you Wednesday," Libby's mother called to my Mom. Libby and I take dance class together after school on Wednesday at the Y.

You have to be careful with William. Once he peed against my leg, thinking I was a tree. I'm afraid he's not that bright.

When we were waiting for the elevator, suddenly Mom gave a jump. "Wow, he's really up and at 'em today," she said.

"She, you mean," I said. If Mom keeps referring to the baby as "he," it might be a "he." I keep telling her that, but she forgets.

I put my hand on her belly to feel. Once I really felt it kick hard. I guess it's getting tired of staying in there just like I did. Well, it's got around three more months to go so it better take it easy!

"Mom, it *is* Rosabelle Franklin, it really is," I said grinning.

"Sure, Toe . . . anything you say."

2

Laundry Day with Dad

Saturday morning is the time Dad and I do the laundry. You see Mom is back in school. It's funny because she went to school for years and years but suddenly she decided to go back again. What she's in is called Law School and on Saturday morning she has a class from ten to twelve. She says that now that she's pregnant, she feels funny when people smoke cigarettes in class. Once she said she almost fainted.

Dad and I do the laundry in our basement. First we go around and take out all the dirty laundry. Most of it is in this big straw hamper in my bathroom. Then we stuff all that in this steel cart we have. Then we gather up this pouch of quarters and dimes that Mom leaves for us. Sometimes she doesn't leave enough and we have to steal from the yellow owl bank in my room.

Our basement isn't that nice. Sometimes I like to imagine I'm a very rich person who's decided to fix up the basement. In my mind I paint all the walls bright blue or white and hang up pictures and put down nice carpets. But, in fact, it's all sort of dingy and gray. We have to stay down there or else someone will take out our wash and put it all in a pile somewhere. Sometimes we have to wait for a dryer. Usually we meet Mrs. Shorr down there.

Mrs. Shorr lives on our floor. She's about the age of my grandma. She *is* a grandma, in fact.

"Hello, Antonia," she said. Dad was stuffing in the wash. "How are you this morning?"

"Okay," I said.

"When are you coming to visit me again, dear?"

I shrugged my shoulders. Sometimes I do visit Mrs. Shorr. She only has two rooms. Her daughter used to live in this building, but she moved. She has three granddaughters, but they're far away. She always gives me things to eat and then says, "Oh dear, your parents will be mad at me . . . they'll think I'm spoiling you." So she rushes over to our apartment and says to Mom, "I'm going to give Antonia some raisins. Is that all right?" Mom always says it is, but the next time Mrs. Shorr rushes over again.

Mrs. Shorr never has much laundry, just a few things. But she waits down there like us.

"Okay, Toe," Dad shouted. "We're all set."

Mrs. Shorr went over to Dad. "You know, Mr. Henderson . . ."

"Chris," he said.

"I don't like to say this . . . but I think it's such a terrible pity when your daughter has such a lovely name, not to use it."

Usually Mom calls me either "Toe" or "Ant." We have a game where I'm Ant and she's Bee. Bea is her real name, actually, Beatrice for long.

"Oh yeah, I guess you're right," Dad said. "Antonia sounds so formal, though, for this devilish creature."

"Antonia is a *beautiful* name," Mrs. Shorr said, beaming. "It's just lovely . . . and I don't consider her a devilish creature at all."

I didn't say anything. Dad likes to tease people sometimes. Personally I hardly know who they mean when someone calls me Antonia. Only Mrs. Shorr does or the teacher at dance class.

"Antonia, you must be so *excited* about the new baby," Mrs. Shorr said.

"Yeah, sort of," I said.

"I was an only child and I was *so* lonely," she said. "I think it's just a *crime* to have only one child."

"Well," Dad said, "I was an only child and I kind of liked it, myself."

"You did?" Mrs. Shorr looked horrified the way she does when Mom calls me "Ant."

"It was fun," Dad said, winking at me.

"I wish people could give birth to dogs," I said suddenly. "I wish I could have puppies." I like to imagine this at times. I'd love to have a whole litter of little puppies.

Mrs. Shorr said, "But babies are so sweet . . . I just *adore* babies!"

Hey, maybe we can give our baby to Mrs. Shorr! "They stink, though," I said. "That's the trouble."

"Stink?"

"You know," I said, thinking of Baby Matilda.

"That doesn't go on forever, fortunately," Dad said. He began taking the wet wash out and putting it in the dryer.

Mrs. Shorr took her stuff upstairs.

"Antonia," Dad said, smiling.

"Oh blah," I said.

"It won't be so bad with the baby," Dad said.

"That's what you think."

"Aida will help out."

Aida is this lady who comes to clean and makes things like veal cutlet for dinner. She grates her own bread crumbs. She doesn't know much English.

"You know, Toe, I have this great idea. I thought you could have that little back room just for you as an extra place once the baby is born."

I thought of that room. It's called a maid's room, but there's no maid in it, just a lot of old boxes and bicycles and stuff. "But it's all dirty and messy."

"We'll fix it up. After the wash we can go to this wallpaper store and you can pick out some you like. We'll put it up and it'll look terrific."

"Ourselves?"

"Sure, it's easy. Then we can put down a new floor."

It was hard to pick at the wallpaper store, there were so many different patterns. I finally picked red and white lions on a blue background. Dad and I started putting it up, but it was harder than we expected. It kept sticking to itself or to Dad.

"God *damn* it," Dad said as the wallpaper swung around and whacked him in the face.

At that moment Mom came home. "Ye Gods," she said. "What's going on here?"

"We're fixing this room up," Dad said. He looked funny with lions all wound around his head.

"It's really hard work," I said. I had on one of Mom's aprons because I was supposed to dust the books.

"It looks it . . . Chris, let Mr. Munt do it."

Mr. Munt is our super. He's a big fat man but he's very good at fixing things.

Dad sighed. "Maybe I better," he said. He climbed down from the ladder.

I went in to sort the laundry. There's a lot you can just fold up and put away like towels and socks. Then every-

16

one takes their own stuff into their room except what has to be ironed.

"Wow," Mom said. "I'm bushed."

Bushed is a funny expression. I think I'll write it in my book of expressions. Mom is always bushed these days. Do you want to know something else that's funny? She doesn't have a belly button anymore. Once last week she was getting dressed for a party and she showed me. "See, Toe . . . my belly button's gone away!"

"Will it come back?" I said.

"Oh sure . . . it did that with you too."

It looks like someone being turned inside out. I can't imagine having no belly button. The person who would mind that the most would be Baby Matilda. She's so proud of her belly button. Whenever I go over to Libby's house she pulls her dress over her head to show it to me and then smiles in this silly way as though having a belly button was so great. Boy, babies are really silly. I bet she doesn't know everyone has one, not just *her*.

3

Something Even
Worse than Twins

Wednesday is a day I've been looking forward to because our dance teacher said the mothers could stay and watch. Up till now they couldn't. That morning Mom brought me down to the lobby. I usually wait there till the school bus comes. When we were in the elevator, we met Mr. Rogo.

Mr. Rogo is a school psychologist. He takes care of little children who don't like school or their parents and things like that. Only I don't like him; he's sort of nosy. This is what I mean. When he saw me, he said, "Hello, hello . . .where are *you* off to so early in the morning?"

Most people would know if they saw a little child in the morning that they were going to school. Anyway, he's seen me before but he always forgets.

"To school," I said.

"What school do you go to, Antonia?"

"New Lincoln."

"And what class are you in?"

"I'm in third grade."

"Oh, how interesting. How old are you?"

"I'll be nine in June."

"Oh? June what?"

"June tenth."

"Well, isn't that *nice*. And pretty soon you'll have a nice brother or sister to play with. What do you want, a little brother or a little sister?"

"Sister," I said.

By then we had reached the lobby and he walked out, smiling.

"You know something, Mom?" I said.

"What?"

"Mr. Rogo is so *nosy*!"

"He's *terrible*," Mom said. "In fact, he's so nosy, I feel like punching him right in the nose!"

I giggled.

"Hey, Ant, I have a great idea . . . next time we see him, you start asking *him* all those questions like 'How old are you? When's your birthday?' That'll fix him. You know what you really should say to him?" Mom lowered her voice to a growl. "Mind your own beeswax, Mister."

We both started giggling. "Ya, I think I'll say that next time I see him," I said. "Mind your own beeswax, Mister," I said in a growly voice.

I knew I wouldn't, it's not good manners, but I wish I could. Maybe I will ask him all those questions back, though. That would be funny.

Mom and Libby's mother sat next to each other during the dance class. Mom looks funny if you're far away from her now that she's pregnant. She looks like the drawings I made when I was little where the person's head would be tiny, but their body would be huge. She looks like there are two babies inside her.

Libby and I did all the usual dancing stuff. The teacher usually doesn't say much, just, "Nice work" or "Try a little harder." At the end we were shooting stars and rushed around with our arms straight out.

After dance class I went to Libby's house. As soon as we got there, who should come rushing out but B.M. She really looked funny. She had two toothbrushes in her mouth sticking out like tusks.

"Help, a saber tooth tiger!" I yelled. "Quick, let's run away."

Libby threw down her coat and ran with me. "Help, help! She's after us! She'll eat us up alive!"

Baby Matilda went running after us, laughing. She doesn't know *what's* going on. Libby's mother said,

"Now girls, settle down." Libby's mother is nearly six feet tall. She has almost no eyebrows, like Libby. Her hair and eyebrows are so light you can hardly see them. She looks like a tree.

Libby and me got on top of her bunk bed, but after awhile we got down because her mother said she had to go to the drug store and would we like to come along and get an ice cream.

I got the kind of ice cream that has a chocolate bar inside. Libby just got a plain vanilla cone. That's all she ever gets! On the way back we saw a really disgusting sight—triplets! They were in this funny carriage, two of them facing one way, the other one facing the other way. I felt sorry for the one facing the other way, but maybe she liked the privacy.

"Maybe your mother will have triplets," Libby said, grinning.

"Oh Lib, stop it! That's mean to say."

Mom is so huge, though. Triplets would be the worst thing in the world. Twins would be awful, but triplets would be so bad I don't know *what* I'd do. "Triplets are very rare," I said. They were moving out of sight. "I don't think Mom will have any."

"Weren't they darling?" Libby's mother said. She was eating a peppermint ice cream cone and holding Baby Matilda by the other hand.

"They were *not* darling," Libby said. "They were yukky."

Libby and me began to laugh.

"Elizabeth, for heaven's sake . . . what a pair of gigglers you two are . . . I've never seen anything like it."

I gave a snort. I always snort when I laugh, I don't know why.

"Tonia's not a giggler," Libby said. "She's a snorter."

That made me snort even more. "I'm going to change B.M. into triplets," I said, "by my special magic wand." I began waving my hands at Baby Matilda. "Woomba, moomba, atala friplets! Turn this baby into triplets!" I gave a jump. "Oh my God, it happened. Look, Lib, there are three of her. Oh, it's terrible. What will we do? I don't know how to change her back!"

"Help, help!" Libby shrieked. "She's triplets. Mom, look!"

"Girls, really . . . you both should enter the foolishness contest for eight year olds."

"We did," Libby said. "We won."

Oh, boy, my side hurt from laughing too much. I tried to get serious again. Maybe Mom really would have triplets!

4

Princess Red Star and
Princess Half Moon
and the Great Campout

Thursday night Libby slept over at my house. We played a really great game. I thought of it. You see, we have this terrace. We don't use it much in the winter because it's too cold, but now that it's getting nice out, we asked Mom if we could sleep out there. She said yes. We got these chairs and draped some blankets over them so it was like a tent. Then under that we put our sleeping bags, right next to each other. We decided to pretend we were Indian princesses sleeping on our reservation. We went into Mom and Dad's room and got some of Mom's

23

lipsticks to use as war paint. We got one orange, one red and one brown. We drew patterns on our faces. Libby looked sort of scary with long brown lines across her forehead and a red star in the middle. That was her name: Princess Red Star. I was Princess Half Moon so I had a half moon drawn on my cheek. I put red circles on my cheeks and some x's near the top of my forehead. Those were scars from antelope hunting. Our tribe lives on wild antelopes.

When Dad came home and saw us, he was amazed. Aida was so scared, she gave a jump. She had her coat on and was just about to go home.

"Who are these wild girls?" Dad said.

We told Dad our names.

"Do you Indian princesses want some hot dogs for dinner?"

"Yes!"

Here was the best part. Mom said we could roast our hot dogs on sticks over the stove, just like it was a real campfire. When we went down to walk William and Elvira, we got some long green sticks in the park. We came home and stuck hot dogs on them. Mom put the fire on low and we stood there, turning them. The stove got a little greasy, but Mom said that was okay.

We brought the hot dogs and potato chips and some orange punch into our tents and ate in there. We pretended William was a wild beast since he kept lurking outside the tent, sniffing the hot dogs.

"We must be very careful or The Wild Beast of the North Mountain will steal our food," I said.

"How long has he been prowling in this neighborhood, Princess Half Moon?" Lib said.

"Since the month of the ripened wheat," I said, finishing off my hot dog.

"The month of the ripened wheat?" said Libby. "What's that?"

"August, dope."

"Oh . . . yeah . . . well, listen, Half Moon, I'm still hungry. How about those marshmallows you said you bought?"

"Follow me, oh Princess of the Empty Stomach. Let us steal quietly to the Great White Room of Many Foods."

We snuck out, throwing a few potato chips to William.

Mom and Dad were eating dinner in the dining room. They eat by candlelight.

"We come for the Marshmallow Feast," I said.

"Aha! The princesses have emerged," Dad said. "Okay, girls . . . let's go to it."

Dad is great at roasting marshmallows. He puts them on the end of a stick, toasts them a nice golden brown, slips off the skin, eats it, toasts it some more, slips off the skin, eats it, and keeps toasting. Libby's kept catching fire and ending up all black and crusty but she said they were good and ate them anyway.

We took a bath but didn't wash our war paint off.

Then we got into pajamas and went out on the terrace.

"You sure you two will be warm enough?" Dad asked.

"Indian princesses feel no cold," I said.

Libby was struggling into her sleeping bag.

The trouble was, it started to rain during the night. And the rain began dripping through our tent. If it was a real tent that probably wouldn't have happened. Libby sneezed, I opened my eyes. There was a trickle of cold water dripping down my nose. It was pitch black out. Probably it was around two in the morning.

"Hey, Lib, let's go inside."

"Princess of Red Star freezing cold," Libby said, sniffing.

"Princess of Half Moon freezing wet," I said.

"You can't be freezing *wet*, idiot."

"Wanna bet?"

We snuck back into my room. The sleeping bags were wet so we pulled out the bed which is under my bed and Lib slept there.

In the morning we slept even later than Mom. She came in at nine and said, "Time to freshen up, Princesses!"

Libby sneezed. "I only slept ten minutes all night," she grumbled.

"Oh, come on . . . you slept *lots* more than that," I said. "I heard you snoring." I felt pretty sleepy myself and yawned.

"I don't snore!"

"Well, you make some kind of funny sound. It sure sounded like a snore to me."

Libby really caught a cold. She didn't even come to school Friday. But when we're grown up, like twelve or so, we're going to do real camping in the forest and stuff like that. That will really be good.

5

Darling Dragon

Usually I don't have dinner with Mom and Dad. That's because most days Dad doesn't come home until seven thirty when I'm about to go to bed. He comes in to say goodnight to me and then he and Mom have dinner. Sometimes I sing awhile, but usually I fall asleep about eight o'clock. But on Tuesday it's different. Tuesday Mom has a class at school from six to eight so Dad comes home early, at five thirty, and we have supper together.

I like having supper with Dad. The good thing is we always have the same thing. With Mom she always wants you to have a healthful meal. She doesn't make you eat everything on your plate like Libby's mother does, but she will give you, for instance, a hamburger with peas and carrots and for dessert applesauce and cookies. With Dad I have my favorite meal: spaghetti and a chocolate malted. Dad has spaghetti too, but he has a glass of beer and some salad.

"This is really going to be a great chocolate malted," Dad said, taking down the blender. I like to tease Dad that his malteds aren't as good as the ones at Baskin Robbins.

"Remember you have to put the ice cream in first," I said.

"Of course I remember that," Dad said. In fact, he doesn't always remember it, but this time he did. Then he added the milk, then the malted stuff and then, "a shot of Bosco," Dad said, pouring it straight from the bottle.

"Dad, at Baskin Robbins they never add a shot of Bosco," I said.

"Never add a shot of Bosco? Nonsense! Of course they do! You can't make a really good malted without a shot of Bosco."

"No, they don't, Dad . . . I *know*."

"I can't believe it. I'm going to go there some time and watch them. You probably don't even notice."

"No, they don't add one," I said, pretending to look sad. "They *never* do."

"Now!" Dad covered the blender and turned it on.

It made a loud whirring sound. Dad always does this funny dance waving his arms at the blender as though he were doing magic to make the malted as good as Baskin Robbins. Then he clicked it off. "Aha! Perfect!" He poured it into a number eight mug for me (we always have mugs with numbers on them going up to ten; I always like to have one of the age I am), added a straw, and we sat down to have our spaghetti.

"Good," I said. "*Almost* as good as Baskin Robbins."

Dad pretended to look sad and tearful. "Just almost?"

"No, it's good, Dad, really . . . only they don't add a shot of Bosco, I know that."

I'm good at twirling spaghetti. Mom said she once saw an ad for a special fork that twirls spaghetti by itself. She said she would get it but she never did. "Dad?" I said.

"Umm?" Dad is not so good at twirling. He mostly bends down and slurps up the ends.

"What if the baby is a boy?"

"What do you mean?"

"It will pee in our faces . . . that's what Libby said."

"Oh, don't be silly, Toe."

"She *said* it."

"He'll be fun after awhile," Dad said. "I bet you'll find it interesting, Toe, teaching him to talk and stuff like that. And if it's a girl, you can tell her everything you know."

"What do I know?" I said.

Dad laughed. "Lots of things! Boy, I didn't know half what you know when I was a boy. I didn't even know how old I was when I was five years old. I remember I had this aunt that always used to ask me and I got so embarrassed because I always forgot."

I had a kool pop for dessert and had my bath. I like to play with my animal soaps in the tub, floating them around on their boat. The trouble is they get mushy that way. When I have a pine bath, I pour the bath water in cups and offer some to everyone. I gave Dad a drink and he said it was delicious. Dad dried me off, but he doesn't rub me with lemon lotion to make me smell good the way Mom does. He just drops my nightgown over my head. But what he does do is give me a piggyback ride into bed. Mom isn't strong enough to lift me anymore, even when she's not pregnant. She's always saying I weigh a ton.

When I get in bed, Dad and me tell our Princess Percival story together. We sort of make it up as we go along, with adding different parts each night. You see, Princess Percival is this princess that has a dragon as a pet. How she got it is this. Once she was supposed to marry this prince if he would slay this dragon that lived behind her castle. But she didn't like the prince at all—he was too fat and had dandruff and bad breath and those things. So in the middle of the night she snuck off and warned the dragon and instead of the prince slaying the dragon, the dragon slayed the prince.

After that Princess Percival and the dragon became best friends. She even came to live in a special yard in the princess' castle. She was really a very gentle, friendly dragon except she liked to eat princes. Princess Percival was so brave she was never afraid of anything. She had a basket of magic snakes in different colors—red, yellow, and purple —and if anyone she didn't like came near, she made her snakes go hissing after them. But she wasn't afraid of the snakes at all. She even wore them around her waist as a belt and let them lick her face with their little forked tongues. Every morning she gave them special milk to drink from a silver bowl.

"Well, today," Dad said, "Princess Percival noticed that her dragon looked a little bit sick. 'What's ailing you, Drag?' she said."

Then *I* continued—" 'Oh me, oh my,' the dragon said. 'I'm pregnant.'

" 'Poor thing,' said the princess. 'When are your babies coming?'

" 'Tomorrow,' said the dragon.

" 'Tomorrow? So soon? You should have told me, D.D.' " (Princess Percival calls her dragon D.D. for Darling Dragon.)

" 'I didn't know,' the dragon said.

" 'Well,' said Princess Percival, 'we must make you a nice soft nest to have your babies in. How many will you have?'

" 'Just one,' the dragon said. 'Dragons always have one.'

"So Princess Percival gathered up the softest straw and silk in her kingdom and made a wonderful nest for her dragon. In the morning, when she got up to brush her teeth, she saw a little bitty dragon curled up at her dragon's side. It was just the size of a walnut."

"A walnut?" said Dad. "So small? I thought dragons' babies were bigger, more like a Saint Bernard."

"No, they're not," I said. "You know, kangaroo babies can fit three in a teaspoon. Well, dragon babies can just fit in a soup spoon. Later they get bigger."

Dad nodded. "Didn't know that, Toe . . . glad you told me."

"Princess Percival knew, of course, because she had read about it in her *Book of Dragon Lore*," I said.

Then Dad said, "Dragon asked, 'What shall I name my baby?'"

" 'Whatever you like,' said the princess."

"I'll name her Percivilla, after you, Darling Princess,' said the dragon.

" 'Why thanks, Drag,' the princess said. 'That's sweet of you.' And she gave her a big kiss.

"Speaking of kissing," Dad added, and he leaned over for me to give him an eskimo kiss. I do two kinds of eskimo kisses—cow eskimos where you rub your nose against someone else's and say, "Mooooo!" and lion eskimos where you rub your nose and say loudly, "Roar, Roar!" This time I gave Dad a lion eskimo.

" 'Night, Dad! Sleep well! See you at seven thirty! Sweet dreams!"

"Same to you, Toe."

6

Saturday Morning

Days I have school I wake up around seven. I get out of bed and play around, but as soon as it's seven thirty I go into Mom and Dad's bedroom. They're usually sleeping, all tucked under their quilts. First I climb on top of Dad and say, "Why, here's big, roly poly nice Dad!" And then I climb on top of Mom and say, "And here's dear little sweet Mom!" Mom is always sleepy in the morning; she just grunts. I say to her, "Time to freshen up!" She grunts some more. Then I hand Dad his slippers which are by the night table. He puts them on and sits there, yawning. It's funny—I always feel peppy when I get up in the morning, but grownups never do, I guess because they go to bed late.

On weekends Mom and Dad like to sleep till nine thirty. I can turn the TV on, though—it's in my room. I have the TV guide in my room, too, so I can see what programs are on. The only thing I can't do is turn on the sound. But that's okay. Sometimes I put on a record and pretend those words are what the TV people are saying, but I have to put it on soft so Mom and Dad don't wake up.

I do whatever I want—crayon or draw, play with my paper dolls, do stuff with my doll house. I even have a play kitchen and I can pretend to make things for my animals. Animals are better than dolls. My favorite ones are Pink Elephant and Mousie, though I like Growly Bear too. Sometimes I dress them up in my old baby clothes and get them ready for a party. I put birthday hats on them and give them cups of punch and everything. I always save party favors from birthday parties I go to, so this morning I gave them all favors too. Mousie got a little compass, Growly Bear got some candles shaped like mice and Pink Elephant got a red address book so he can write his friends' names down.

At nine thirty I went into Mom and Dad's room. But a funny thing happened—they weren't there. The bed was all messy, but no one was in it. That's never happened before in my whole life. They never get up early on Saturday. I went into the kitchen, thinking they must be there making breakfast but the only person there was Aida. She was cleaning up like she always does, with her apron on.

"Where're Mom and Dad?" I said.

Aida knows Spanish mostly. If you talk to her in English, you have to speak slowly. She said, "They go to hospital . . . baby comes . . . baby start to come."

I stared at her. "But it's not *supposed* to come. Not till June."

Aida shrugged. "They go . . . they be back later."

How come they went if they're coming back? I couldn't figure it out. I went back to my room to play some more, but I didn't feel that much like it. So I got dressed and went back in the kitchen. "Aida, I'm going to take William and Elvira for a walk," I said.

I've never actually taken William and Elvira for a walk alone, but I don't think Aida knows that. She looked at me and said, "You don't want breakfast?"

"I'll have some chocolate milk," I said and she fixed it for me.

"That's your breakfast?" she said.

"I'll get some other stuff later," I said.

William was lying right near the door, pointing straight at it, like an arrow. You could tell he wanted to go out because when he saw me, he began jumping all around and licking me. Even Elvira began to whine and nudge against me. I put on William's leash and we went down.

It was warm out, nice and sunny. William gave such a lurch to the curb that he practically made me fall over. He really had to pee badly. I was glad I thought of taking him down. I decided to go just to the end of our block. With Mom I sometimes go into the park, but I knew she wouldn't want me to cross the street myself.

About halfway down the block we met a lady with a German shepherd. William is always very friendly with other dogs. In fact, he rolls right over on the sidewalk and gets his leash all tangled up, he's so glad to see them. Elvira is just the opposite. She almost always growls, even if it's some huge dog that could bite her in two if it wanted. That's never happened, however. There's only one dog she likes, another Yorkshire terrier named Sasha that lives one block down.

"Are those *both* your dogs?" the lady said while William was rolling around.

I nodded. Elvira was off her leash so maybe the lady thought she was just taking a walk by herself. "What's *your* dog's name?" I said.

"Morris," the lady said.

"How old is he?"

"Eight years old."

That's pretty old for a dog, middle-aged anyway. "He doesn't *look* that old," I said.

"No, he thinks he's a puppy," the lady said, laughing.

It's funny that people are always saying about dogs, "He thinks he's a puppy" or "He thinks he's a person."

It seems like most dogs don't think they're just plain dogs.

"I never saw you before," I said.

"No, we're new on this block," the lady said. "Do you like it?"

"Do I like what?"

"Do you like living here?"

"We've always lived here," I said.

"Oh," said the lady, "so you're a city child."

I nodded. "Only we go to Fire Island on weekends."

When I got home, I wrote the name of her dog in my Dog Book. That makes twenty-two dogs I have so far. You see, every time I meet someone with a dog, I always stop and ask its name and age. I hope I don't seem like Mr. Rogo, too nosy, but I do it for a reason. My reason is that when I get older, I'm going to have the job of being a dog walker. Once I saw a girl walking six dogs, some big like William, some very small like Elvira. Mom said that girl goes to the houses of those people and they pay her to walk their dogs. I had this other idea which is that maybe I could take a lot of dogs to Fire Island one summer and look after them for people. I could sleep on the porch and the dogs could have my room. They would love the beach. I could hose them off on hot days and play ball with them. I would get a lot of money but I would also like it. So I have my Dog Book just so when I'm old enough, I will know which dogs I would like best to have. Some dogs just don't have nice personalities. I would only take the ones I really like.

While I was sitting there, writing down Morris and looking over the other dogs in my book (I always draw a picture of the dog too, as well as I can, so I'll remember what he looked like), I heard the key in the lock. It was Dad.

"Where's Mom?" I said, running out in the hall.

"She's in the hospital," he said. He looked sort of tired. He took off his coat. "She had the baby," he said.

"What kind?" I said.

"A boy."

I didn't say anything. I guess a boy might not be so bad. I'll just have to see.

Dad stood there not saying anything for awhile. Then he said, "It's having trouble breathing, Toe . . . he's so small, you see."

I nodded.

"They think he'll be all right, but . . . he shouldn't have come so soon."

"I *know*," I said. "Why did he?"

"Those things just happen." Dad yawned. "Listen, Toe, I'm going to take a nap, but later I'll have to go back to the hospital, so I thought maybe I'd take you over to Aunt Marjorie's on the way. Maybe you can sleep there. Could you pack a couple of things?"

"Wow! Yes!" I said. I just *love* sleeping at Aunt Marjorie's. I took down my bag and packed a nightgown and a clean dress and my toothbrush. Dad went in and closed the door to his room. In a few minutes I could hear him snoring. Here's a funny thing: Elvira snores too!

Sleeping at
Aunt Marjorie's

Aunt Marjorie is my mother's sister. She's twenty-four; my mother is twenty-nine. I love Aunt Marjorie's apartment. She lives in a little building, not a big one like ours. She lives on the second floor and you have to walk up to her apartment. Her apartment is just one big room with a kitchen at one end. It has everything in it—a bed, a table, a couch that turns into a bed. When I grow up, I want to live in an apartment just like that.

Aunt Marjorie has a job. She decorates store windows. Once Mom and I saw her, standing in the window dressing a plastic lady. She has wonderful hats that she lets me try on and three boxes of jewelry that I can spread out. When we go to shows, she lets me wear whatever of her jewelry I like. Once I wore three pins all at once.

From her boy friends Aunt Marjorie gets nice presents which she sometimes gives to me. Once she gave me a stuffed snake which I named Jimmy Sebastian. Last time she gave me a candle shaped like an owl. She said she wasn't going to see that boy friend any more so he wouldn't mind.

"Sorry to barge in like this," Dad said to Aunt Marjorie when we got there.

"Don't be silly, Chris!" Aunt Marjorie said. She was in blue jeans and a funny shirt with crocodiles on it. She has red hair like carrots and freckles. Mom only has freckles in the summer; Aunt Marjorie always has them. "Keep me posted," she said when Dad left.

"Tonia, you're just the person I was hoping would come over today," Aunt Marjorie said.

"What do you want me to do?" I said. Sometimes Aunt Marjorie wants me to do things like paint her bathroom with her or help her make a necklace out of shells.

"We're going to do some painting," she said. She showed me how for one of her store windows she wanted it to look like summer and we had to paint lots of leaves all different colors. The leaves were already cut out of paper, hundreds of them. Aunt Marjorie had this special shiny paint and she wanted me to paint each one a differ-

ent color. She said in the end it would look like a real
tree, because real trees are not just green, they're all different colors. I thought that only happened in the fall,
but Aunt Marjorie said no. She gave me an old smock
to put on.

"Aren't you lucky to have a brother?" she said while
we were painting.

"I was hoping it would be a girl," I said.

"Girls are nice," she said, "but a little brother might
be fun to take care of."

I painted a leaf purple. "How come *you* don't have
children, Aunt Marjorie?"

She laughed. "I don't have time," she said.

"Will you ever have them?"

"Maybe."

"When I grow up, I'm just going to have one child,"
I told her, "a little girl."

"One is good," Aunt Marjorie said. "I think I'll have
one too."

"One . . . two," I said. "You can't have one *and* two.
You have to choose."

"I choose . . . you!" Aunt Marjorie said. She had a
spot of blue paint on her nose.

When we were finished painting, we spread the leaves
out on the floor. There were so many they covered almost
the whole floor. We had to close the window so they
wouldn't blow around. Then Aunt Marjorie said we
should go out until they dried. We decided to see *Mary*

Poppins. I saw it once already, but I wanted to see it again. Here's a funny thing with Aunt Marjorie that I never saw with anyone else. She falls asleep in the movies. She says she can't help it. She starts to watch and then her eyes close and pretty soon she's asleep. Mom said she always did that, even when she was a little girl. I say— why go then? But she says she likes it. She says she sleeps better in the movies than anywhere else. I just *knew* she would sleep at *Mary Poppins*, even though there's a lot of singing and dancing. That never bothers her at all.

When we got out, it was getting dark. Aunt Marjorie gave a yawn. She said we could eat in or out, whatever we wanted. I said out.

"Let's go to that place where they play the guitar," I said.

"That's not really a restaurant, but, okay, sure," said Aunt Marjorie.

Aunt Marjorie can play the guitar. So can her friend, Michael, who plays at this place called The Café Geronimo which is near where Aunt Marjorie lives. You can tell him what to play and he will play it.

"I want spaghetti and a chocolate malted," I said when we sat down. It was so dark you could hardly see till you got used to it.

"No malteds, Miss," said the waiter. "Just spaghetti."

"Okay . . . spaghetti and water," I said. Aunt Marjorie had a cheeseburger. She's quite thin.

We sat and listened to Michael play the guitar. He's really going to be a doctor but he likes to do this best. He said when I was nine, he would come to my birthday party and play songs. When I get older, Aunt Marjorie is going to teach me how to play the guitar. She says you have to have tough fingers. Hers are very tough so they don't mind plucking at the guitar strings. When you touch the tips, they feel hard and round, like dog paws.

When we got back to her apartment, the leaves were all dry. One thing was that some of them weren't as shiny as they had been when they were wet. But Aunt Marjorie said tomorrow we would shellac them to make them shiny. There was a painty smell so we opened the window. We put all the leaves in a straw basket.

"Bath time, Tonia," Aunt Marjorie said. She knows I love to have a bath at her house. The reason is that she has wonderful soaps, all different colors and smells. One is red and smells like a tomato, one is shaped like a lemon and smells like a lemon. There's a cucumber one and one like nuts. "What flavor will it be tonight?" she asked.

"Lemon," I said.

Lemon made me think of Mom since she always rubs me with lemon lotion after my bath. I hadn't really missed her till now, but suddenly I felt very sad, as though I wanted to cry. I stayed in the tub a long long time playing a game and pretending Growly Bear, Pink Elephant, and Mousie were there. They have a friend named Soup who is shaped like a potato who comes to visit them sometimes.

When we were in bed, Aunt Marjorie brushed her hair. She lets it hang over so you can't see her face.

"Would you like to brush it for me?" she said.

I did it for awhile, but I got tired.

"How about a bed time snack, Tonia?" she said.

I felt so sad I didn't even feel hungry. I just snuggled down under the covers. At home I have these phosphorescent stars on my ceiling that I like to look at when I'm falling asleep but at Aunt Marjorie's there aren't any.

"When will you get up in the morning, Aunt Marjorie?" I said in a whisper.

"Oh, I don't know . . . you just shove me when you want me to," she said.

I wonder what our baby will be named. I hope Theodore with Teddy for short. I told Mom that's my favorite. She likes Hugo but that makes me think of a seal. Dad likes Mark but there are too many Marks already. It's almost as bad as Peter. I have three Peters in my class! Teddy would be the best.

Tomorrow I'll tell Dad to tell Mom.

8

Appletopiness

In the morning, just while I was brushing my teeth, the phone rang. Aunt Marjorie who was still in bed answered it. She talked for awhile and then said, "Tonia . . . your Dad is coming to pick you up."

"But we didn't shellac the leaves yet."

"We can start doing it till he comes."

We had some cereal and then we sat at Aunt Marjorie's table, painting the leaves with shellac. Shellac is no color, but it makes things shiny. The leaves looked the way shells do under water. Sometimes at Fire Island I collect these stones and shells, but they only look really beautiful under water. You can make people out of stones by gluing them together and drawing faces on them with a dri mark pen. Mom and me do that sometimes and we add beards out of cotton and stuff like that.

Dad came at ten o'clock. "Oh Dad, let me just finish the leaves!" I begged.

"I have a cab waiting," he said in a strict voice. "Now get moving, Toe."

Usually Dad isn't strict. I made a face which I don't think he saw and went to get my suitcase.

In the cab Dad didn't say anything, he just sat there looking out the window and drumming his fingers on his knee. I began looking at the cab driver's ticket up in front. His name was Alphonso Minigetti. What I like to do is see if the cab driver looks the way you'd imagine due to his name. I close my eyes and imagine what I think he will look like. Then I look at him and see if I'm right. I imagined Alphonso Minigetti would have a black moustache, long and droopy, and a big nose and maybe snow white hair. Well, he did have a big nose but his hair was black. He was more a father than a grandfather. There's a dog named Alphonso on our block. He's a puli, which is a kind of Hungarian sheep dog, and he's the only puli I ever met.

Upstairs William began jumping around and barking when we came back. "Shut up, William!" Dad said.

"He needs to go out," I said.

"Well, he can wait five minutes."

William and I looked at each other in surprise. Dad is not usually like that.

Dad went into the living room and sat down. He said, "Come here, darling."

I came in.

Dad said, "You see, puss . . . the baby died."

"Our baby?"

He nodded.

I felt like I couldn't swallow, like I had something stuck in my throat. The corners of my eyes felt wet. "He was too small, I guess," I said after awhile.

Dad said, "Right . . . he just . . . his lungs weren't developed enough. He couldn't get the hang of breathing."

I sat down. "That's too bad," I said.

Dad sighed. "Of course, Mom feels especially terrible," he said. "It's the worst for her, carrying him around in her all these months. It's as though on Christmas Santa Claus brought you no presents even though you'd been good, that's how she feels only maybe even worse."

I could imagine how bad that would be. "When will she come home?"

"In a few days. She has to rest a little. She might be a little sad when she comes home so we have to be especially nice to her."

I nodded. "I can draw her some pictures. Maybe I'll make her a book."

"That would be nice, Toe." Dad smiled. "Sorry I was so grumpy before."

"That's okay," I said.

"Are you hungry? Do you want anything to eat?"

I shook my head.

Dad said, "I'm kind of beat, Toe. I think I might take a nap. Do you want the TV in your room?"

I nodded. Nothing is on that much Sunday afternoon, but I decided to have it anyway. There's a special at seven about The Cat in the Hat which I guess I'll watch. I have the book about him.

The house was so quiet after Dad went to take his nap. Aida wasn't there, no one was there but us. Sunday is a quiet day, of course, but this was almost too quiet.

I went inside to call Libby. I know her phone number by heart. She answered the phone.

"Oh Toe!" she said. "Now what do you *want*? I was just in the middle of doing something."

Sometimes Libby can be very bossy on the phone. "What are you doing?" I said.

"Making some more clothes for Regina." Regina is a huge paper doll Lib has who has a wardrobe of eighteen dresses, some trimmed with real sequins and fur and things.

"Oh."

"So, what do you want to say?"

"There's a special of The Cat in the Hat tonight," I said.

"I *know*!"

"Are you going to watch it?"

"Of course!"

"Well . . . see you, Lib."

"Toe?"

"What?"

"I made up a new word this morning."

"What is it?"

"Appletopiness."

We both giggled.

"So long, Toe."

"Bye, Lib."

I decided to tell Libby about the baby in school tomorrow.

I went back to my room. Now I would always be an only child. That's what I wanted. There won't be any baby to pester me. I'll have my room all to myself. But I felt bad somehow. I guess I really had gotten used to the idea of the baby coming. I was sort of planning for it in my mind. In the beginning I thought if I was God or something like that I would make Mom not pregnant, but now I think I would make that baby come alive again. I wish I could. Mom must feel really bad.

I decided to make her a book about Ant and Bee with faces like me and her, but bodies like real ants and bees. I drew some pictures and then stapled them together. I decided to get Dad to write the words later. I can write, but it takes a long time and I didn't so much feel like it.

If the baby had been born, I would have gotten presents probably. I wonder what they would have been. Libby got a new present every day her mother was in the hospital with Baby Matilda. One day she got a record of someone telling stories. Another day she got a doll that can say ten things if you pull a string. But it fell off her bunk bed and now it doesn't say anything. Then I think she got some other stuff, a new coloring book or something. I wonder what Dad was thinking of getting me.

I put my Christmas carol record on and went to the kitchen to get a snack. The cookie tin was almost empty, just some old fig newtons which I hate anyway. I hate that figgy taste. When I came back in my room there was Dad.

"How come you're playing carols?" he said. "It isn't quite the right season."

"I like them," I said.

I went into the bathroom and sat on the hamper while Dad shaved. He has an electric shaver that makes a buzzing sound. When he shaves in the morning it makes the TV get funny, all wavy.

"Dad, we're low on cookies," I said.

"We're low on a lot of stuff, Toe," Dad said. "We better go to Pioneer."

Pioneer is open on Sunday. I love to go there. Usually I go with Mom on Sunday if we run out of something which we usually do. I don't think I ever went there with Dad.

"Why don't we call Mom and say hello to her?" I said.

"Why don't we do that later, hon? I think she's probably sleeping."

"Okay."

9

Mom Comes Home from the Hospital

My school bus picks up Libby after me. We always sit in the back. We trade turns on who gets the window.

"Libby, my mommy lost her baby, you know," I said.

"What do you mean? You can't lose a baby," Libby said. "Did she go to the Lost and Found?"

"It's just an expression," I said. "The baby died. He was born too soon and was too small."

Libby nodded. "I heard of that happening."

"It's sad," I said.

Libby shook her head. "Boy, you're really lucky, Toe

. . . I mean it! Now you'll always be an only child just like you wanted."

"I know."

"I wish we could give Baby Matilda to someone. You know what she did this morning?"

"What, Lib?"

"She ripped up the cover of that new book I got. Just for no reason . . . and she spilled honey all over Christabelle." (Christabelle is Libby's tiger.) "Now she'll have to be shampooed and everything."

"Baby Matilda?"

"No, Christabelle. You're the luckiest person I ever heard of. Boy!"

I guess I am quite lucky, but I felt really mad at Libby. She could at least say she was sorry or that it was sad or something. Just because Baby Matilda does those bad things doesn't mean *our* baby would have. Our baby might have been really nice. I didn't say one thing more to Libby till lunch time. If someone dies, you should at least be sorry. It's different if I used to say bad things about Mom having a baby. It was *our* baby so I can. But you shouldn't with someone else's baby. That's just mean. Dying is the saddest thing that can happen to someone. You'd think Libby would know that.

I spoke to Mom on the phone after school.

"How's everything doing, Ant?"

"It's okay . . . I'm sorry about the baby, Mom."

"Oh . . . thanks, darling. I do feel sad, but . . . well, we'll see."

"What was his name?"

"I hadn't decided yet."

"I thought Teddy would be good."

"I know you did, hon. Ant, I miss you."

"I do too . . . miss you, Bee. Will you really be home tomorrow?"

"Umm . . . when you come home from school, I'll be there."

"I have a surprise for you, Bee."

"Oh good, darling. I can't wait to see it."

When I came home from school that afternoon I rushed into Mom and Dad's bedroom and there was Mom, sitting up in bed, reading the newspaper. She looked the same. Probably she was thinner than when the baby was in her but you couldn't tell so well since she was partly under the covers. She was wearing a nightgown and bed jacket. I guess she just washed her hair because it was all wrapped up in a towel.

I jumped up on the bed and hugged her. "Oh Mom!" I yelped.

Mom hugged me back. "Oh Ant! I'm so glad to see you." Her towel began slipping off. "Whoops."

I put my hand on her stomach. It was still a little fat, but not like it was before. It was sort of loose and pouchy. "I'm sorry about the baby, Mom."

Mom shrugged. "Ya, well . . . " She suddenly smiled. "I can start another one pretty soon. It's not the end of the world."

"Another one?" I was so surprised. I didn't know you could just start another one like that.

"No reason why not," Mom said. She picked up the book I had left for her. "I like your book, hon."

"Oh, but listen, Mom, I didn't do the writing part. I meant to, but I didn't have time."

"Maybe we can type it later."

"Hey, could we? Really?"

Sometimes Mom and I go into Dad's study and I dictate to Mom. That means I tell her what to type and she types it up. Then we cut it out and paste it on the other side of the drawing so it's like a real book.

"Right now I'm still a little sore," Mom said, "but maybe tomorrow. Ant, do you want the TV in your room? *The Electric Company*'ll be on soon. Or, wait a minute, I'm not positive I can lift it. Let's watch it together in here."

So I snuggled up in bed next to Mom and we watched *The Electric Company* together. I was so glad Mom was back. The worst time of missing her was that time at Aunt Marjorie's. Otherwise it hadn't been so bad, but it was still better when she was back.

"How did you and Dad fare while I was away?" Mom said.

"What do you mean?"

"Did everything work out all right? Did you have enough to eat?"

"We went to Pioneer," I told her. "We got all the stuff there."

Dad came home early, at five thirty. He had a big bunch of lilacs for Mom. Those are her favorite flowers. For me he had a new set of phosphorescent dri marks and a new nonsense coloring book. Phosphorescent means they glow in the dark. It was nice that I got some presents even if we didn't have the baby.

Mom said she would just eat in bed because she was still tired, so Dad and I fixed her this tray. Here's what she had: poached eggs on toast, spinach, a cup of tea, and canned pears for dessert. I helped Dad cook everything. You have to pat off poached eggs when they come out so they aren't too wet. Otherwise the toast gets soggy. We pulled a chair up near Mom's bed and she ate off the tray.

Dad and I ate together in the dining room. I had spaghetti and a chocolate malted. Boy, I've had spaghetti and a chocolate malted practically every day this week. I never had it that much before. For dessert we went into the bedroom and had it with Mom.

"How are you feeling, Mom?" Dad said.

"Okay, Dad," Mom said. "The lilacs are lovely. Did you smell them, Ant?"

I smelled them. They were good. Dad gave me a little bunch to put in my room.

Mom stayed in bed most of that week. Every day

when I came home from school, she'd be in bed reading and I'd come in and we'd watch TV together. I lent her my new coloring book. Mom loves to color; she never goes over the lines. The trouble was she almost filled in the whole book. But she said she'd get me another one. By the end of the week she was in a regular dress again. But one day when I came home, when I went into the bedroom she was crying.

I felt so funny. I didn't know mommies ever cried. When she heard me, Mom looked up and began sniffing and saying, "Oh Ant . . . is it three already?"

I pounced on her and began patting her. It made me so sad to see her cry I thought I might cry. "Don't cry, Mom."

"I won't, Toe . . . I don't know why I did. It's silly . . . I should get out really."

"Are you still sad about the baby?" I said. Sometimes if I think about the baby my eyes feel wet at the corners.

She nodded. "I guess. But I know we'll have a baby some time. So I shouldn't . . . Toe, let's take William and Elvira down, okay? I think I just need some fresh air, that's all."

Mom and I went down with William and Elvira. In the elevator we met Mr. Rogo.

"I was so sorry to hear about your misfortune," he said.

Mom just looked at her feet. I thought about what we had planned about telling Mr. Rogo to mind his beeswax, but I decided this wouldn't be a good time to say anything.

"Did Elvira ever have puppies, Mom?" I said when we were in the park.

"No, Toe, she never did. Only once, it was funny, she had this thing called a false pregnancy."

"What's that?"

"Well, it's when a dog wants to have puppies and be pregnant but isn't but she starts giving milk anyway and her nipples hang down."

"Did Elvira do that?"

Mom laughed. "Yes, I used to have to milk her every morning."

"Really?"

"Yup, she had real milk in her nipples . . . poor old thing."

"Maybe she should have had real puppies."

"Maybe. Now she's too old, though. And in a city apartment it's hard. It's easier if you have a yard."

When I grow up, I'm going to have a yard so I can have lots of animals, not just dogs but cats, birds, turtles, everything. It's much nicer for William and Elvira in Fire Island. Except last summer people got mad at William for peeing on their lawn. Also, he used to wait around for people's groceries to be delivered and then he would sneak food out of the bag. Once he stole three steaks from somebody's grocery bag and they got so mad, they said they would shoot him!

But they never did. He really couldn't help it. He just loves to eat so much. It's not really his fault.

10

Fire Island

The best thing that you can eat is steamed clams. On Fire Island you can get them all the time. School let out in June and now it's almost halfway through the summer. I go out with Dad and we just dig around with our toes and when we hit one, we pull it out. Dad even eats them raw sometimes, but they look so slimy. I would never do that.

"Umm, it smells marvelous," said Mom. She was sitting in the living room in the rocking chair with a blanket over her knees. She's going to have another baby.

That's what she said. It's already there, in her stomach. She had said she wouldn't go clamming because it was too dank out. I like the word dank. I like it when words sound like what they mean.

"It wasn't dank," I said. "It was nice."

"It was nice, dank clammy weather," Dad said, dumping the whole basket of clams in a big pot.

"Honey, do you need any help?" called Mom.

"No, you stay where you are. I have all the help I need right here at my elbow."

It's fun when Dad and I take over in the kitchen. He's sort of messy—he doesn't clean things up right away, but I like it.

"How do you feel?" he called in to Mom.

"Fair to middling."

"Still queasy?"

"It's getting better."

Queasy is another of those words that sounds like what it means except I don't like what it means.

I went in to Mom and sat on her lap. She pulled the blanket around me. I put my hand on her stomach. "I can't feel anything," I said.

"Well, darling, of course not . . . it's much too small. You won't be able to feel him till September or so."

"Can you feel him?"

"No."

"Then how do you know he's there?"

Mom thought a minute. "Well, the doctor can tell.

And I'm getting fatter. And, being queasy, that shows he's there."

"I wonder if *he* feels queasy," I said. I wonder if he likes clams. "Is it the same baby?" I said.

"The same baby? What do you mean?" Mom said.

We were all warm and toasty together like that, as though we were one person. It was nice. "The same baby as the one that died," I said.

"Well, it can't be the same," Mom said. "How could it?"

"Why not?"

She frowned. "I don't think that can happen. I mean, it's always different . . . like snowflakes are always different."

"I think it's the same baby, coming back."

"Darling, it can't be, it just can't."

Maybe it can't. But how do they know? Maybe it can. Why shouldn't it come back? It could die and then decide that if Mom was having another baby, it might as well try again. Why should it give up after just one time?

When I was little, I imagined the inside of a mommy's stomach was like a waiting room with benches and all the babies were sitting there. But when it came time to come out, they would all shove to the front, only one would make it out. If two made it out, then it would be twins. But then the door would close and they'd all have to wait until next time.

"Clams!" yelled Dad.

Mom stretched and yawned. "I am so darn hungry," she said. "What's wrong with me? I just think of eating all the time."

"Libby's mother said she gained sixty pounds every time she was pregnant," I said, sitting down at the table.

"She couldn't have!" Mom said.

"She was pretty fat, I guess," I said. The clams were really good. "She's quite tall, though."

"Still." Mom looked at Dad. "Don't let me get enormous, Chris, okay?"

"Of course not," said Dad. "Toe and I will chase you around the house every day ten times if you start getting too fat."

I guess most people end up having two babies. There's nothing you can do about it. They have one and then they figure that one was so nice they want another one. Of course, if that one was bad, maybe they would not want to have another one.

It's nice in the summer. I like it, even if Libby is away. I told her she could come up for the weekend, but it's odd, she gets scared if she sleeps away from home. I sort of know what she means. Last summer I slept at this girl Marilyn's house out here on Fire Island and in the middle of the night I got up and walked home. I'm glad I knew where to go. But if Libby came, she couldn't just walk home to New York City. She'd have to wait for a ferry.

I didn't tell Libby about the baby yet because she said

those mean things when the first one died. If she says one mean thing, she's not going to be my best friend anymore, no matter what. And that's final.

I took a bath after dinner and then read in my room. My room here is really small, sort of like that maid's room we have at home. I don't mind it. I pretend it's the cabin of a boat and the window is a porthole. At nine o'clock I got up and went out in the living room. They let me stay up pretty late here. They don't even notice sometimes that it's nine o'clock.

They were sitting on the porch. Dad had his arm around Mom and they were just sitting there, looking out.

"Boo!" I said, suddenly leaping into Dad's lap.

"Who can this be?" he said.

"It can be no one but me," I said.

"Toe, I'm too tired to move . . . let me say goodnight to you here," said Mom.

I said, "Good night, sleep tight, sweet dreams, see you at eight o'clock . . . your turn!"

Mom said, "Good night, sleep tight, sweet dreams . . . see you at eight o'clock." That's the way we do it. Mom has to say it after me, then Dad. I don't sleep well if they don't say it.

Dad tucked me in. "William Pincus takes showers with his mom and dad," I said.

"He does?"

"Yes, and I want to too."

Dad sighed. "I don't know, Toe . . . I'll have to think about it. Maybe you can do it with Mom."

"No, I want to do it with you!" I said.

"I don't think we'd better," he said.

"Why?"

"I guess I'd just feel embarrassed."

"Why?"

"I guess I just wasn't brought up like that. My mother would have fainted if I'd even asked her that."

"Really?"

"More or less."

It seems like daddies never want to do it. Libby's dad wouldn't either. They just think if you see them without their clothes on, you'll faint or something. Well, I wouldn't. I saw William Pincus pee right on the beach yesterday and I didn't faint at all. Boy! Grownups really get these funny ideas.

II

The Big Blackout

"Girls, I'm afraid you're going to have to come to the beauty shop with me," Libby's mother said. "It shouldn't take too long."

"Can we get comics?" Libby said, "so we'll have something to read."

"Oh, okay." My mom and dad won't let me buy comics, they say they're stupid, but Libby's mother lets her. Anyway, we like going to the beauty shop. Libby and I are big now—we're in fourth grade. We even put eye shadow on sometimes. When Henrietta Zuckerman had her birthday in September, there were these eye shadows in our loot bags.

"Will you put nail polish on us?" Libby asked the lady who runs the beauty shop.

"Libby, don't be a pest," said her mother.

"Why is that a pest?" said Libby. "That lady is having it."

"That lady has an appointment. Now read your comics as long as you bought them."

Baby Matilda was at home with a baby sitter. You'd be amazed at how Baby Matilda has changed this year. I couldn't believe it. She's almost like a regular person. She knows millions of words! When I was at Libby's house, she was looking at this word book she has and Baby Matilda knew all the flowers on the flower page. She knew really unusual flowers like Sweet William and Pansy and Fox Glove. I never thought she'd turn out that smart. She doesn't even smell any more because she's toilet trained. She still makes mistakes sometimes, though. Once in the playground she peed right in her tights and got them all wet. Libby's mother said, "I knew you shouldn't have had that load of ginger ale, Mattie." But Baby Matilda just took off her tights and was okay.

Libby and I read our comics and then we watched while this lady had nail polish put on her. I decided I would like Pink Passion on my nails if the lady who runs the beauty shop would do it. Libby said she wanted Paint the Roof Purple. Purple seems to me a yukky

color for nails, sort of like eggplant. Anyway, the lady wouldn't do it. She said we could just have a dab of this color that was just regular, like skin. Still, at least she did something.

Libby and I sat on the floor and waited for it to dry.

"I don't mind that we're having a baby that much," I said. I'd already told Libby we were going to.

"Yeah, they always have them . . . you can't do anything about it, anyway," Libby said. "They think they're so cute."

"Baby Matilda is better," I said. "She seems pretty good."

"Sometimes," Libby said. "But she still loses a lot of stuff like Chinese checkers. She just puts them in her trucks and then you can never find them. She practically ruined my whole set!"

I felt my nails to see if they were dry. They were still sort of gummy. "I wonder if we'll have the same baby," I said.

Libby stared at me. "What do you mean—the same baby?"

"Well, maybe that same baby, the one that died, maybe we'll have him again."

"You can't do that! That baby died!"

"But maybe he would want to come back."

"That doesn't matter. Even if he did, he can't. If you die, that's all there is to it. You can't come back."

"How do you know?"

"I just do. You don't believe in angels and stuff like *that*, do you?"

"No, but, well, I just don't see . . . they don't really know . . ."

"They do so! Boy, that's the stupidest thing I ever heard!"

I didn't say anything. Probably Libby is right. It will be a different baby. Anyway, that's okay. Who says the one that died was so nice? Maybe the new one will be better. But I still don't see how they know, really.

All of a sudden, right while we were sitting there, a funny thing happened. All the lights started to go out. All the hoods that the ladies were under stopped making this whirring sound. It was scary. The lady who runs the beauty shop opened the door and out on the street it was dark too. When she came back in, she said, "It's a blackout."

"What's that?" Libby whispered. She looked really scared. Libby hates the dark. She won't even let you close the closet door if you're in there with her.

"There must have been a power failure," said Libby's mother. "We better go home." She looked funny walking out on the street with these big rollers on.

"I don't want to go home!" Libby yelled. "I'm scared."

"Libby, for heaven's sake," said her mother. "Now just hold Tonia's hand and my hand and stop your blubbering."

The word blubbering is funny, but Libby was too

scared even to laugh. We weren't far from Libby's house, just a few blocks. But when we got there, we had to walk upstairs. It was sort of exciting in a way. People were going up the stairs with candles.

"I hope Mrs. Zuckerman has kept her head," Libby's mother said.

"Kept her head?" said Libby. "Where would she put her head if she didn't keep it?" It was the first time she had talked since we left the beauty shop.

"I mean, I hope she didn't panic," said Libby's mother.

It was pitch dark in Libby's house too. Mrs. Zuckerman, the baby sitter, was right there at the door and so was Baby Matilda. Libby's mother hugged Baby Matilda. "Mattie, puss, little baby face . . . how are you?"

"Fine," Baby Matilda said. "It's dark."

"We know it's dark, dum dum," said Libby. "We're not blind."

"No lights," Baby Matilda said. "Lights go out."

"Boy, this is really great," said Libby. "I can't even see *anything*."

"I wonder if we have any candles," Libby's mother said. "I wonder where they would be."

She began looking for candles. Libby and I went into her room.

"Hey, maybe it'll be dark for the rest of our life," Libby said.

"People will have to wear special phosphorescent clothes," I said, trying to imagine that.

"They say the power should return at eight o'clock," said Mrs. Zuckerman who was in the kitchen listening to this little radio she had.

"I hope Daddy can come home," Libby said. She had a funny expression.

"Lib?"

"Yeah?"

"Are you still scared?"

"Not so much. It's funny . . . I can see pretty well now."

"Me too."

"Girls!" Libby's mother called. "Would you please help me look for the candles? I know I stashed them away somewhere."

Libby and I began looking in the dining room, but we couldn't find them.

Then all of a sudden Libby's mother said, "Why look at that! Mattie found the candles. Good work, Mattie. Where were they?"

"In the closet," Baby Matilda said.

"How did you remember they were there?" Libby's mother said. "Smart girl. How do you like that, Libby? Mattie found the candles."

"Terrific," Libby said.

"Mattie is a smart girl," Baby Matilda said.

"Don't boast," said Libby, but I think she was glad, too, that we would at least have candles till the lights went back on again. It was just like Halloween with everything dark except for the light from the candles. We let Baby Matilda play with us and be a ghost while we were Halloween cats. We did that till the lights went on and then I went home.

12

Libby's School Birthday

Most people have two parties for their birthday. They have a school birthday and then a regular one. For the school one the mother comes with cupcakes and candy. Last year our teacher, Mrs. Prensky, wouldn't let us have candy, even for our birthdays. She was really strict. But this year Mrs. Hoffman says we can. Mrs. Hoffman is young and she has a husband. We know because he once came to school. He had a moustache.

Libby is going to be ten on March third. She always gets to be her age before I get to be mine. For the school birthday you don't have party hats or favors or anything like that. The mother just comes at lunchtime with cupcakes. Then she has lunch with our class. They make a special place for her, usually next to her child. Then she comes out with cupcakes for dessert with some candles in the one for the person who has the birthday. Then that person blows out the candles and makes a wish. Oh yes, and of course we sing "Happy Birthday to You" and "How Old Are You?" That's all there is. You don't get presents or anything. Some people don't even have a school birthday if they were born in the summertime. Libby says Baby Matilda will be like that since she was born in the end of June.

For your real birthday at home you just invite your special friends. They don't even have to be from your school, if you don't want. You can have some from camp or dancing class or anything.

"Well, I'm not having any boys, I can tell you that," Libby said.

"You did last year."

"Well, I'm not this year. Zachary Weissberg threw up at my party last year."

"I thought that was because he ate too much candy."

"It was. He's such a pig. I don't even like him anymore."

"I like Freddy Lifton," I said.

"So, marry him, then."

"I didn't say I wanted to *marry* him . . . I just said I liked him."

"He's okay. But for my party I'm just going to have girls."

Maybe I'll do that for my party too, I don't know. It isn't for three more months anyway.

Libby's mother looked in the door. "Now girls, please remember, don't go around talking about Libby's party at school. It's not fair to those who aren't coming."

"Oh, we know that," Libby said.

"Maybe we should have the whole class," Libby's mother said.

"I don't want the whole class," said Libby. "That's what the school birthday is for."

"Yeah, I guess it would be sort of a madhouse," Libby's mother said. "How many cupcakes do you need, Lib? Eighteen?"

"Yes, and I want all different flavors like Henrietta Zuckerman had."

"I know, I know."

The day of Libby's school birthday I wore a quite new dress. You're not supposed to wear a real party dress but you can put ribbons on your pigtails if you feel like it.

"What'd you get, Libby?" Henrietta said when Libby came in that morning.

"Barbie's Country Camper," Libby said.

"I have that already," Henrietta said. She always says

that. She has practically every toy you ever heard of. Only Libby and I don't like her so much. She's too bossy. Like if you play with Sara Abudo, Henrietta will say she won't be your friend any more because she doesn't like Sara. She does stuff like that all the time.

"Your camper is broken already," Libby said. "But I'm going to lock mine up so my baby can't even touch it. I'm only going to play with it when she's asleep. She'd just wreck it."

Henrietta doesn't have a baby in her family. She just has a brother who's quite old, twelve or thirteen or so.

At lunch time we all came downstairs to the lunchroom. Libby's mother was there. She's so tall her head almost touched the ceiling. But she sat next to Libby and ate sandwiches with us. Libby doesn't eat at school that much. She doesn't even like peanut butter and jelly sandwiches. All she likes is french fries. Mom says she will fade away if that is all she eats, but she hasn't so far.

Libby's mother went in to get the cupcakes. Then a lady came from the kitchen to call Mrs. Hoffman to the phone. When she came back, she said with a smile, "Your father is on the phone, Tonia."

I went in back and lifted up the receiver.

"Toe . . . we did it! We have a little brother for you!"

"Already?" I said. Mom had been at home when I left for school.

"Yes, he just slipped right out in no time at all. Mom was awake during the whole thing."

"Can I speak to her?"

"Well, she's resting now, honey. But I just wanted to let you know right away."

"Is he nice?"

"He's gorgeous. Wait till you see him. He looks about a hundred years old. Babies always do."

I giggled. "They do?"

"All except the fat, double chinned ones . . . like you were."

"Oh Daddy!"

"See you later, puss."

When I came back into the lunchroom, Mrs. Hoffman stood up and said, "I have an important announcement to make. Tonia now has a baby brother! Her father just called from the hospital."

Everyone began to shout, "Yea! Hurray!" My heart started beating really fast, I was so excited. Libby looked extremely mad. She glared at me. I guess she thought I had spoiled her birthday by having it happen right then.

"How come it happened *now*?" she whispered.

"I don't know . . . it just did, I guess."

Then Libby's mother brought in the cupcakes and Libby blew out the candles but I could tell she was still sort of mad.

"Well, how exciting!" Libby's mother said. "I bet you can't wait to see him, Tonia."

I nodded. "I wish they would let me go right now and see him."

"They never let you see them," Freddy Lifton said. "It's stupid. They won't let children go to the hospital."

"My mother had her baby at home," Sally said. "I watched."

Mrs. Hoffman looked surprised. "Did she really, Sally?"

"It only took fifteen minutes," Sally said. "She just pushed and pushed and it came right out."

"Oh boy, I wish I could watch," Freddy said.

"Me too," I said.

"If my mother has another one, I'm going to ask her to do it at home," Freddy said.

"Most mothers feel more comfortable in a hospital," Mrs. Hoffman said.

"Hey, I have a good idea," Freddy said. "You get pregnant, Mrs. Hoffman, and have your baby at school. Then we could all watch."

That sounded like a really good idea, but Mrs. Hoffman said she wasn't sure. She said she'd have to think about it.

After school I went to Libby's house. I was so excited I could hardly play or anything. I kept wondering what they would call him. When Libby's mother had Baby Matilda, she sent us a postcard to Fire Island, saying, "I had another No Name Monster" and for a long time Libby and I used to call Baby Matilda No Name Monster, even after she got her real name.

"It may not be so bad," Libby said. "If you were an

only child, you might get bossy. And you'd get spoiled."

"No, I wouldn't!"

"You might ... without knowing it. What do you think your father will get you? Probably a baby doll. That's what they always get you."

"Maybe he'll get me Barbie's Country Camper."

"Oh boy! That's *too* good! You're not supposed to get that unless it's your birthday." Libby looked mad again. I guess she felt jealous.

In three days I'll see the baby. I hope he's cute. I hope I like him. But mostly I hope he's a nice person when he gets to be big like me.

13

Baby Brendan

We named him Brendan and he's three months old now. He's not so bad, but he doesn't do much yet. He sleeps in that back room, the one Dad and I got fixed up. He seems to like the lions on the wallpaper. He points at them and makes sounds. He might be trying to roar, it's hard to tell. When he first came home from the hospital, he used to wake up in the middle of the night and cry. But now he sleeps through. Only tonight I heard Dad getting up and I woke up. I can tell it's Dad because he wears bedroom slippers that make this padding sound. Mom goes in her bare feet.

Dad is the one who gets up to give Baby Brendan his bottle at night. He says Mom should get her rest. I got out of bed and went into the little room. Dad was just sprinkling Baby Brendan's behind with powder.

"Toe, what're you doing up?" Dad said.

"Just woke up," I said. "How come he did?"

"He might be teething," Dad said. "I think his teeth are bothering him."

Baby Brendan has these beads to chew for his teeth, but he's always dropping them and then you have to wash them off. Dad put a clean diaper on him and then carried him over one shoulder into the kitchen. He got a bottle out of this box of bottles. He put a nipple on it. Then he went into the living room. First he put on his raincoat. Dad always wears his raincoat when he feeds Baby Brendan because once Baby Brendan spat up all this milk over Dad's new suit.

"I think this fellow is hungry," Dad said, sitting down in the arm chair. "Aren't you, fatso?"

Baby Brendan just snapped onto that bottle and began to drink. He really is amazingly fat. I think he should be on a diet. He has four chins. I'm not exaggerating. I counted them once. And he's fat all over. He can hardly fit in his clothes, he's so fat. Mom and Dad think he's cute.

"Dad, I think he should drink skimmed milk," I said. "Look how fat he is!"

"Oh, he'll slim down," Dad said. "You were fat too, Toe."

"Not like *that*!"

"Yes, you were. Lots of babies are. It goes away."

I don't believe I was ever that fat, I just don't. I think Dad just doesn't remember.

In the middle of feeding him Dad stood up and walked up and down the room with Baby Brendan slung against him. Baby Brendan doesn't even open his eyes when he drinks. It's hard to imagine you can sleep and drink at the same time, but that's what he does. Dad walked up and down with him, back and forth, until Baby Brendan gave this very loud burp. For a person that would be rude, but for a baby it's okay.

"Good boy," Dad said. "Toe, want to give him the rest of the bottle?"

I went to get my raincoat. Baby Brendan never spat up on me, but, as Dad says, there's no point in taking any chances. I sat down and held him in my lap. He snapped right onto that bottle again. He's like William —he's always hungry. I gave him my finger and he curled his hand around it. He likes to do that. He has such funny little hands, fat, with round little fingers. He opened his eyes and smiled, but went right on drinking.

Dad yawned. "I'm going to get myself a snack," he said. "Want anything, Toe?"

"Maybe some roast beef," I said.

One thing I like to eat in the middle of the night is cold roast beef bones.

Baby Brendan finally fell asleep so I put him back in

his crib. You have to put him on his stomach, but when you come in in the morning, he's rolled on his back. He likes to look at this mobile hanging over his crib. It's of eyes, all different colors.

Dad and I sat in the kitchen eating our bones. "Wow, I was starving," Dad said.

"It's funny that if we didn't wake up, we wouldn't even know we were hungry," I said.

We had some pickles and crackers and hard boiled eggs. It was a real midnight feast.

"Next summer Baby Brendan will be walking, I bet," I said.

"Maybe sooner," Dad said.

"When he's one year old, I'm going to teach him to talk," I said. "I'm going to make him practice every day."

"That's a good idea," Dad said.

"Dad?"

"Umm?"

"Will we have more babies?"

"I don't think so, Toe. Two is a lot, I think. Why, would you like more?"

"Well, I always thought it would be nice to have a sister," I said.

"I think we better stop while we're ahead," Dad said.

"Are we ahead?" I said.

He smiled. "Sure!"

We put the stuff back in the refrigerator. Then we

took off our raincoats. Dad tucked me in. "Sleep tight, darling."

"You too, Dad."

Those stars on my ceiling are getting dim. I never noticed it till now. Maybe I'll climb up on a ladder and paint over them. I might put some up in Baby Brendan's room. I bet he'd like stars.

NORMA KLEIN's reputation for perceptive and honest explorations of a youngster's world has grown ever since the publication of her celebrated first book for children, *Mom, the Wolf Man, and Me.* She is the author of more than twenty books for children, young adults, and adults, including the recent title *No More Saturday Nights.*

Ms. Klein is a graduate of Barnard College and holds an M.A. degree in Slavic languages from Columbia University. She lives in New York with her husband and two daughters.

4656